You Know It!

SAMMY
the Steiger

Gotcha!

FRANKIE
the Farmall

Go[t It!]

CODY
the Combine

Hey Dudes!

BAILEY
the Baler

Go Team!

KELLIE
the Combine

Awesome!

PETER
the Patriot Sprayer

VROOM!

SCOOTER
the Case IH Scout

Let's Do It!

TAMMI
the Tiller

Details!

EVAN
the Early Riser Planter

This book belongs to:

Name: _ _ _ _ _ _ _ _ _ _ _ _ _ _

Favorite cookie: _ _ _ _ _ _ _ _ _ _

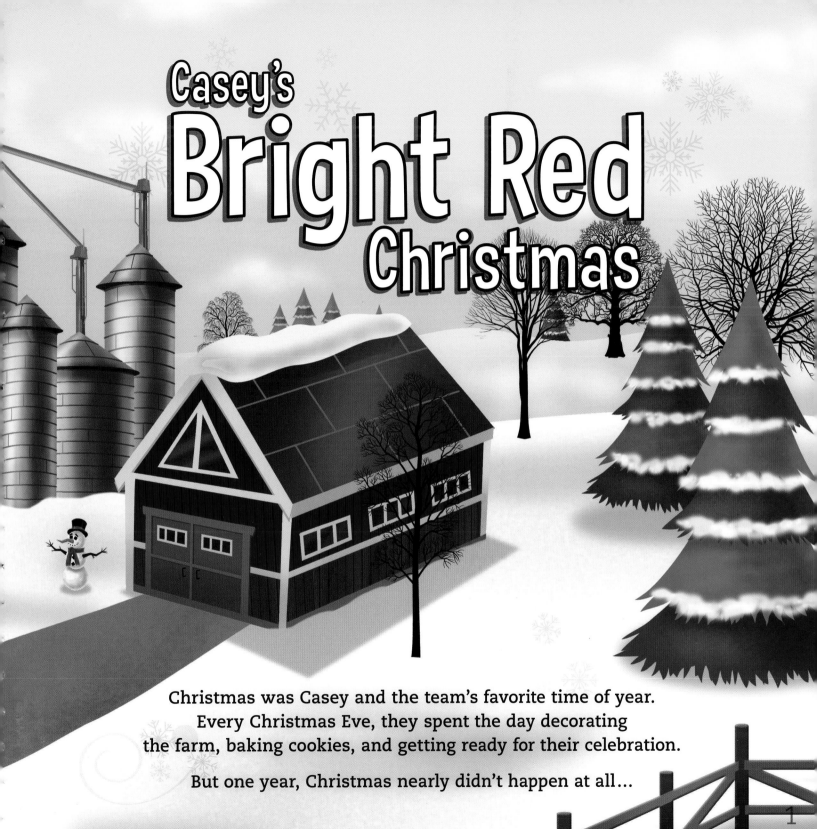

Casey's Bright Red Christmas

Christmas was Casey and the team's favorite time of year.
Every Christmas Eve, they spent the day decorating
the farm, baking cookies, and getting ready for their celebration.

But one year, Christmas nearly didn't happen at all…

"Good morning, Tillus," Casey greeted her friend as she finished breakfast. "What's the weather forecast for today?"

"It's going to be a great Christmas Eve—bright and sunny," Tillus answered. "The team is ready to begin the Christmas fun!"

2

"I almost forgot what day it was," Casey said with a sniffle. "First I need to do my chores." Then she sneezed. "A-choo!"

"Are you feeling all right?" Tillus asked, looking concerned.

"It's nothing, just a little cold," Casey answered. "Now let's get to work. I want to finish as quickly as possible so we have lots of time to decorate."

3

"Good morning, ladies," Casey said to the cows as she walked into the barn. "Are you ready for breakfast?" In response, the cows began mooing. "Your stall needs to be cleaned out and replaced with fresh straw, too." She sneezed and sighed. "There's always something to do…"

Looking around the barn, Casey noticed a box with Christmas lights poking out of it. "So that's where I put that box of decorations," she said. "I better take it to the shed after finishing up here. The team is probably looking for it."

5

Once her work in the barn was finished, Casey walked to the shed.
On her way, she noticed a board on the fence was broken.
"I'd better fix that before it gets any worse," she said to herself.
Grabbing her tools, she set to work. Just beyond the fence,
Casey noticed the trees were glittery with snow.
"I still need to cut down the Christmas tree," she reminded herself.

After Casey fixed the fence, she began working in the shed.
"I'm ready to plow snow." Frankie zoomed up to her. "Where should I begin?"

"You can start in the farmyard," Casey replied. Then she sneezed.

"Are you feeling OK?" Frankie asked.

"I'm fine. It's just a little cold," Casey sniffled. On the worktable,
Casey noticed the team's Christmas stockings lying in a heap.
She had taken them out last week, but never had a chance to hang them.
"I've got to get those hung before tonight," she said to herself.
"There's so much to—'a-choo'—do."

Thinking about her chores, Casey listed the jobs she needed to finish. "I still need to change Big Red's filter, order seed for spring planting, and organize the tools." She turned to see Frankie plow nearby. "I hope there's enough time to get ready for Christmas, too," she said quietly, thinking about all of the things she'd rather be doing with her team.

Inside her kitchen, Casey warmed up some soup for lunch.
"You've been working so hard lately," Tillus said when he saw his tired friend.
"Now that your chores are finished, why don't you take a nap?"

"I want to spend the rest of the day with the team. It's our tradition to decorate Happy Skies Farm together." But even as she said this, Casey yawned and her eyes drooped. "I'll join you and the team outside in just a minute." Instead, Casey fell fast asleep at the table.

13

Inside the shed, Tillus gathered the team together. "Where's Casey?" Kellie asked, looking around. "We can't start decorating without her."

"We always spend Christmas Eve with her," Fern agreed.

"Casey isn't feeling well," Tillus explained. "She fell asleep after lunch."

Everyone began talking at once. The thought of spending Christmas without Casey was unthinkable. Maybe this year, Christmas should be cancelled. "Wait a minute," Tillus called out. "Casey takes care of us throughout the year. It's time for us to take care of her."

"Yes," Big Red said with a smile. "Let's give Casey a Christmas surprise she'll never forget!" The team cheered in agreement. Then, they went to work.

Fern and Frankie began decorating the shed with lights.
"Um… Frankie. I need your help!" Fern called.

"In a second, Fern. I just need to hit Cody with these snowballs!" Frankie answered.

Big Red and Sammy found the perfect Christmas tree.
"Follow me, Sammy. My bright red nose will lead us home!" Big Red said.

"Maybe your GPS should lead us home instead," Sammy replied.

19

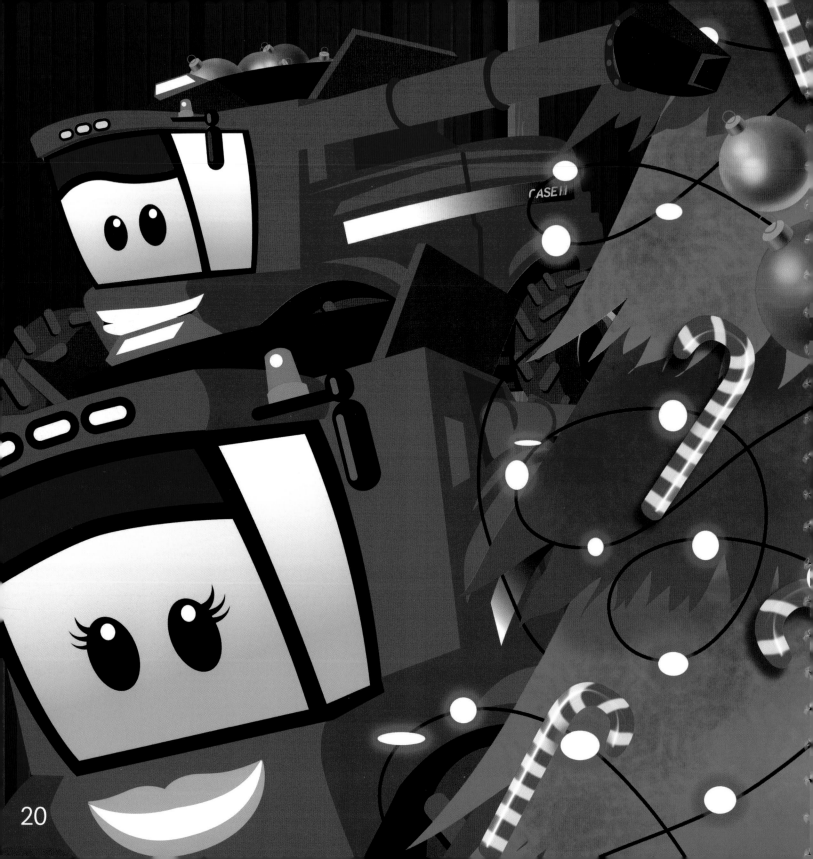

Cody, Kellie, and Peter decorated the Christmas tree.
"The tree could use more ornaments over here," Kellie said.

"Everything looks better with glitter!" Peter sang.

21

Tillus, Tammi, and Evan tried their best to make Christmas cookies.
"Do these cookies have too much frosting on them?" Tillus asked.

"There's more frosting on you than that cookie!" Tammi answered.
Meanwhile, Evan continued to place exactly one sprinkle on every cookie.

Inside the shed, Bailey wrapped hay bales for the cows.
"Dudes, these bales are wrapped nice and tight!" he exclaimed.
"Here come more!" Frankie added.

25

Casey woke with a start. "Oh no! I can't believe I fell asleep."
Outside the window, Casey saw twinkling lights. She could hear
Christmas carols and laughter, too. "What's going on?" she wondered.
She quickly rushed outside to find out.

"Surprise!" everyone shouted as Casey entered the shed.
Casey looked at each member of her team as tears welled up
in her eyes. "Everything is beautiful," she said.
"Thank you for the best Christmas gift I could ever imagine!"

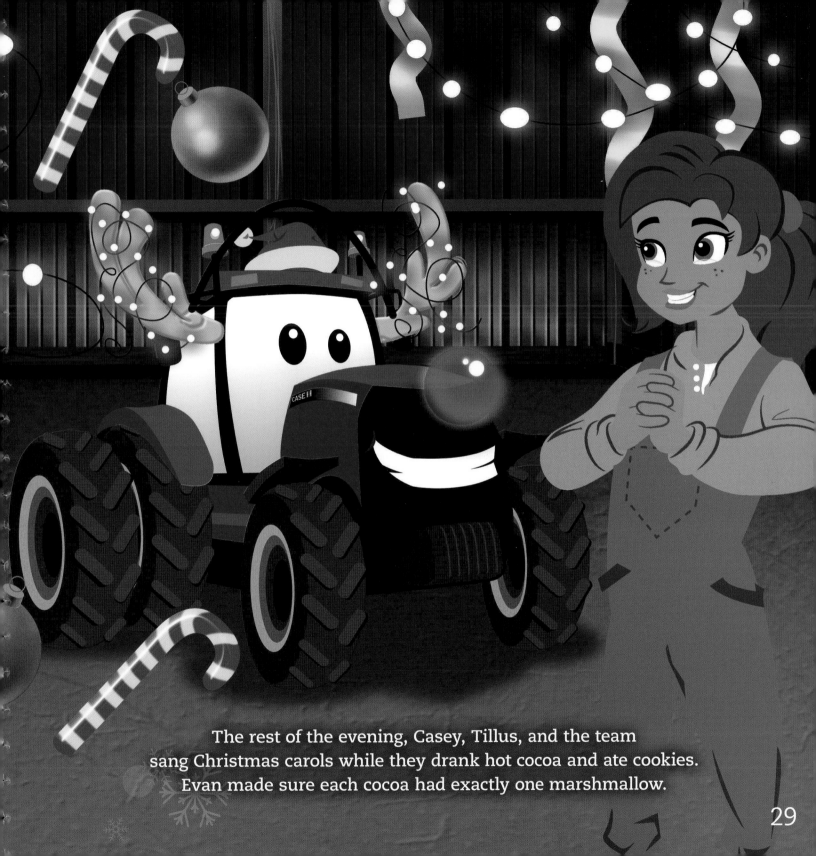

The rest of the evening, Casey, Tillus, and the team
sang Christmas carols while they drank hot cocoa and ate cookies.
Evan made sure each cocoa had exactly one marshmallow.

"Merry Christmas!"

Irma Harding® Frosted Sugar Cookies

Cookies

2 cups all-purpose flour, plus more for rolling out cookies

1 ½ teaspoons baking powder

¼ teaspoon salt

¾ cup butter

¾ cup sugar

1 tablespoon + 1 teaspoon milk

1 teaspoon vanilla

1 egg

Mix flour, baking powder, and salt together. Set aside.

In large bowl, cream butter, sugar, milk, and vanilla until blended.

Beat in egg.

Add flour mixture until blended.

Divide dough in half, shape in rounds, and wrap in wax paper.

Refrigerate at least 1 hour or overnight.

Heat oven to 375° F.

On floured surface, roll out dough to about ¼-inch thick and cut out cookies with floured cookie cutters.

Place 1–2 inches apart on ungreased cookie sheet.

Sprinkle with colored sugars or other decorations. Leave plain to frost when cool.

Bake 7–9 minutes until light, golden brown around the edges.

Cool slightly and move to cooling rack.

Makes 2–3 dozen, depending on size and shape of the cookies.

Frosting

1 cup powdered sugar

½ teaspoon vanilla

2 ½ to 3 tablespoons milk or water— vary to produce desired consistency.

Add a few drops of food coloring for colored frosting. This can be done in small batches to provide a variety of colors.

Octane Press, Edition 1.0, October 1, 2015

ISBN: 978-1-937747-61-9

Library of Congress Cataloging-in-Publication Data

1. Juvenile Nonfiction—Transportation—General. 2. Juvenile Nonfiction—Lifestyles—Farm and Ranch Life.

3. Juvenile Nonfiction—Lifestyles—Country Life. 4. Juvenile Nonfiction—Concepts—Seasons

Library of Congress Control Number: 2014954286

octanepress.com

Printed in the United States

Farming keeps me busy, but I love my life!

CASEY
the Farmer

Casey depends on me for the daily weather report!

TILLUS
the Worm

Easy Peasy!

FERN
the Farmall

Be Ready!

BIG RED
the Magnum